Juneteenth
★ FOR MAZIE ★

FLOYD COOPER

PICTURE WINDOW BOOKS
a Capstone imprint

Published by
PICTURE WINDOW BOOKS
a Capstone imprint
1710 Roe Crest Drive, North Mankato, Minnesota 56003
www.mycapstone.com

Library of Congress Cataloging-in-Publication data is
available on the Library of Congress website.

ISBN: 978-1-4795-5819-3 (library binding)
ISBN: 978-1-4795-5820-9 (paperback)

Summary:
Mazie is ready to celebrate liberty. She is ready to celebrate freedom. She is ready to
celebrate a great day in American history. The day her ancestors were no longer slaves.
Mazie remembers the struggles and the triumph, as she gets ready to celebrate Juneteenth.

Designer: Russell John Griesmer

Special thanks to Dr. Kenneth W. Goings
Professor of African American and African Studies, The Ohio State University

Printed in the United States of America in North Mankato, Minnesota.
122019   003040

"For the Williams, the Banks, the Perkins,
and the Cooper families — the clans that form my tree."
—*Floyd*

Mazie wants to play outside, but it is too late.
"It's getting dark, Mazie. It's time to stay inside."

Mazie wants a cookie, but it is time for bed.
"Not now, little one. It's too close to bedtime."

Mazie wants to stay up late, but she is too little.
"Bedtime is the rule, sweet girl."

"Why so grumpy, Sugar Bear?" asks Dad.

"I can't go where I want, have what I want, or do what I want," answers Mazie.

"Well, tomorrow you can have a celebration," says Dad.

"What are we celebrating?" asks Mazie.

"We will celebrate the day your great-great-great-grandpa Mose crossed into liberty! The day will be celebrated by us and many more families on a day we call Juneteenth."

Dad lifts Mazie into his arms.

"I bet you're tired of hearing 'no' all the time. Well, Great-great-great-grandpa Mose heard 'no' even more."

"Grandpa Mose worked in fields that stretched all the way to sunset. He and the other slaves would be bone tired, but they had to keep going. Their masters wouldn't let them quit. But as they worked, they thought about freedom."

"And before they finally went to sleep at night, they prayed about freedom and made plans for change and a better future.

Some slaves ran north to freedom, following a bright star in the sky."

"They sweat, they bled, and they cried till those cries were quieted by a single proclamation from a brave president. Grandpa Mose heard that proclamation read from the balcony of the hotel on that warm June day in Galveston, Texas."

"Grandpa Mose heard nothing but cheers, saw nothing but happiness, and felt nothing but pride shared by all those around him. The cheers became dancing. The dancing became celebrating. It went on and on into the night."

"Grandpa Mose and the others had found freedom. They continued to work, but this time they were paid for their hard work. So they worked. And they saved. And they never forgot the moment they heard — the moment that changed their lives forever."

"But things weren't perfect. Black people still struggled to stand shoulder to shoulder with white people. They still weren't treated as equals. It wasn't easy, but they never gave up. And every year on Juneteenth, they remembered."

"They marched for jobs. They lobbied
for schools and the right to vote.
They shouted for opportunity."

"And every year on Juneteenth,
they celebrated and remembered."

"They learned and they grew . . ."

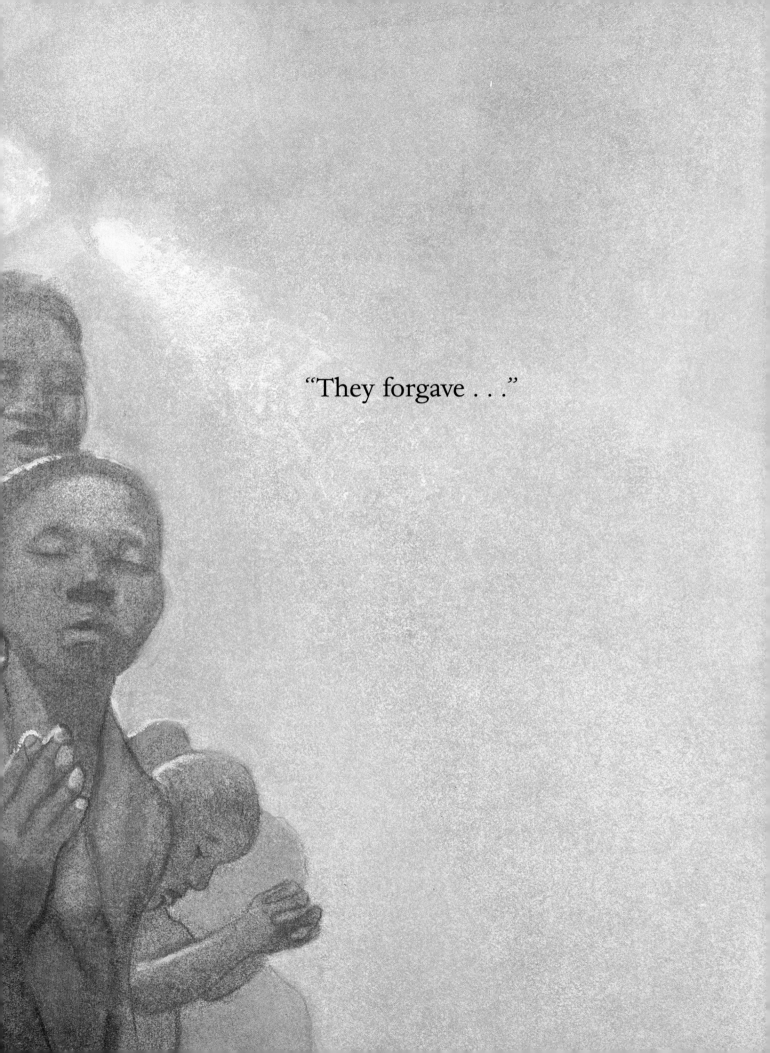

"They forgave . . ."

"They excelled and achieved.
They became heroes . . ."

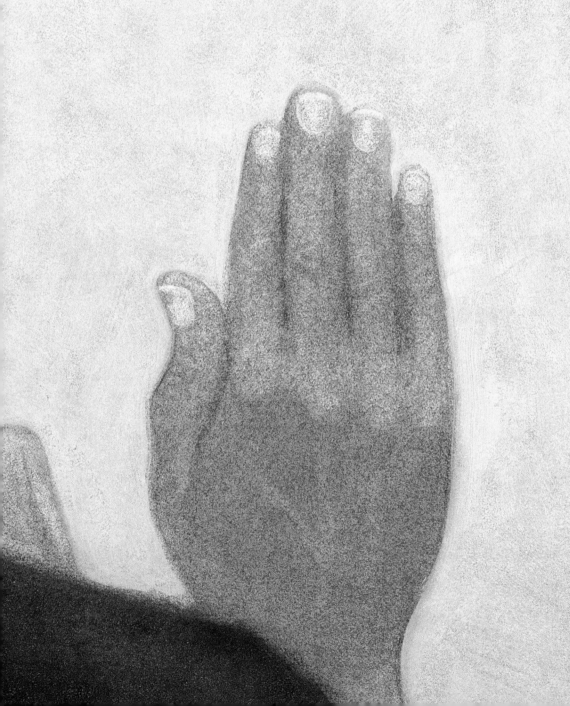

"Now, sweet Mazie, it's your turn to celebrate just like Great-great-great-grandpa Mose."

"It's your turn, Mazie, to eat some barbecue and drink some strawberry pop."

"It's your turn to celebrate . . ."

"... and to remember."

On June 19, 1865, soldiers arrived in Galveston, Texas, announcing the end of the Civil War and the end of slavery in the United States. It was more than two years after President Lincoln's Emancipation Proclamation. Celebrated every year on June 19, Juneteenth commemorates the announcement of the abolition of slavery and the emancipation of African-American citizens throughout the entire United States.